To Scott and Chris
-D.A.

For Mama, Baba, and Dana
Thank you, Jesus, my Lord and Savior.
-K.L.

Published by
PEACHTREE PUBLISHERS
1700 Chattahoochee Avenue
Atlanta, Georgia 30318-2112
www.peachtree-online.com

Manufactured in April 2012 by Imago in China
10 9 8 7 6 5 4 3 2 (hardcover)
10 9 8 7 6 5 4 3 2 1 (trade paperback)

Illustrations created in acrylic on paper. Text typeset in ITC Zemke Hand.

Library of Congress Cataloging-in-Publication Data

Adams, Diane, 1960-
  Zoom! / written by Diane Adams ; illustrated by Kevin Luthardt.-- 1st ed.
     p. cm.
  Summary: Illustrations and rhyming, easy-to-read text describe a father and child's
wild ride on a roller coaster.
  ISBN 13: 978-1-56145-322-0 / ISBN 10: 1-56145-332-3 (hardcover)
  ISBN 13: 978-1-56145-683-3 / ISBN 10: 1-56145-683-7 (trade paperback)
  [1. Roller coasters--Fiction. 2. Stories in rhyme.] I. Luthardt, Kevin, ill. II. Title.

PZ8.3.A213Zo 2005
[E]--dc22
                              2004016710

ZOOM!

Written by
Diane Adams

Illustrated by
Kevin Luthardt

DINO COASTER

PEACHTREE
ATLANTA

"Here's your ticket. Step inside. Are you tall enough to ride?"

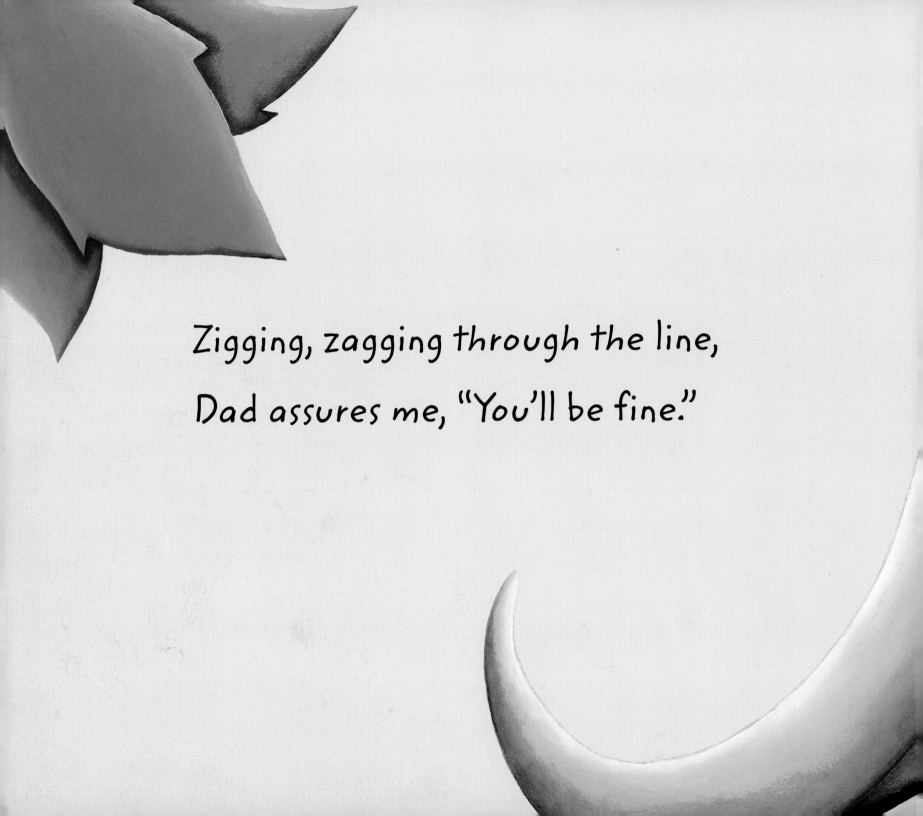

Zigging, zagging through the line,
Dad assures me, "You'll be fine."

"All aboard," the crewman cries.

I lock my seatbelt, close my eyes.

Click-click-clacking up the track.

Sinking lower, peering back.

Slowly climbing to the top,
Edging closer toward the drop.

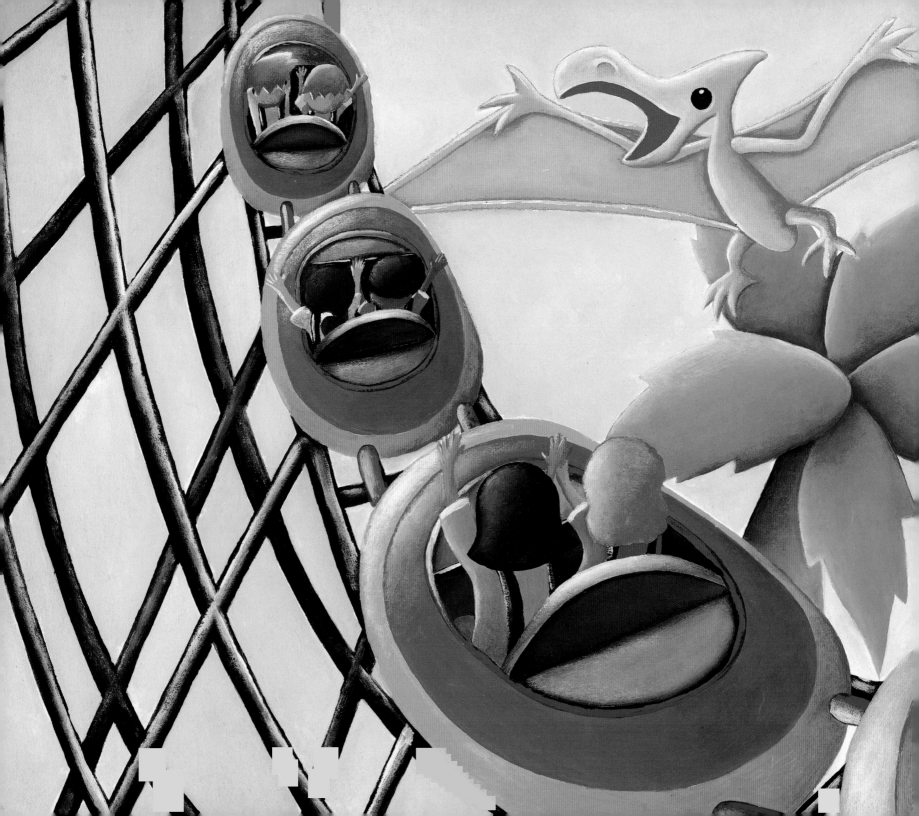

Sailing at the speed of sound.

Zooming, racing toward the ground.

Lurching, tilting up again.

Jerking, rumbling round the bend.

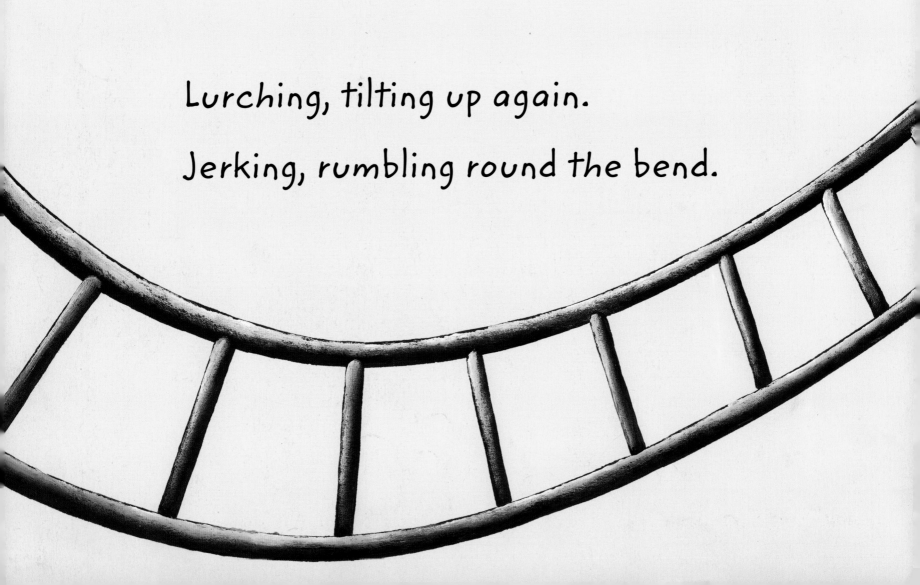

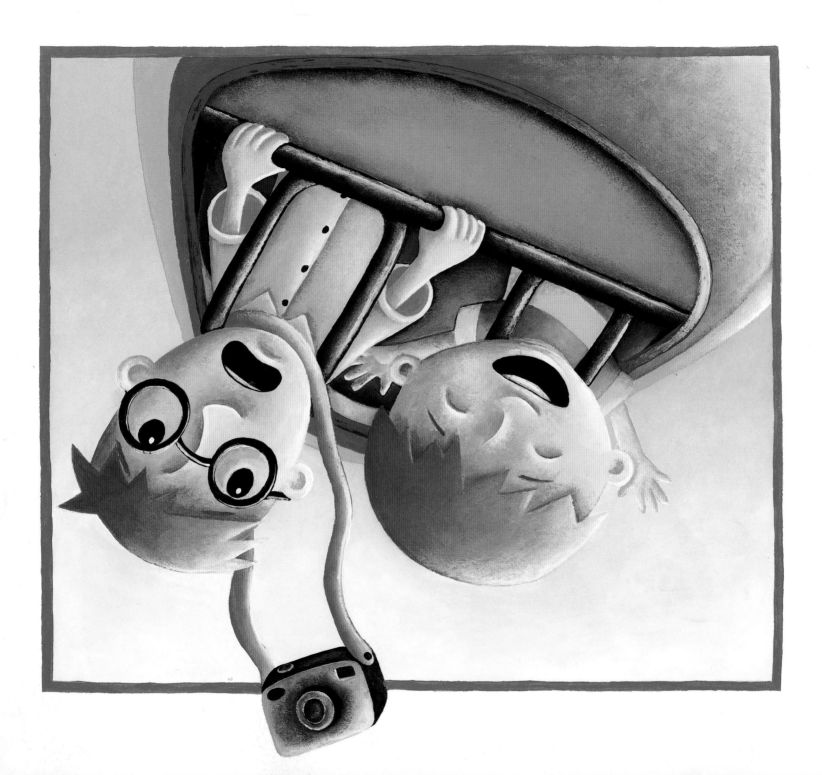

Backward, forward,

Upside down.

Crashing, splashing,
Twisting round.

Slipping, sliding, holding fast.

"How much longer can this last?"

Creaking, squeaking, slowing down,
Seatbelts loosen. Feet touch ground.

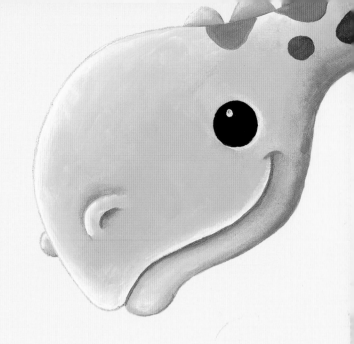

I race out with Dad behind...

Grab a ticket.

Stand in line!

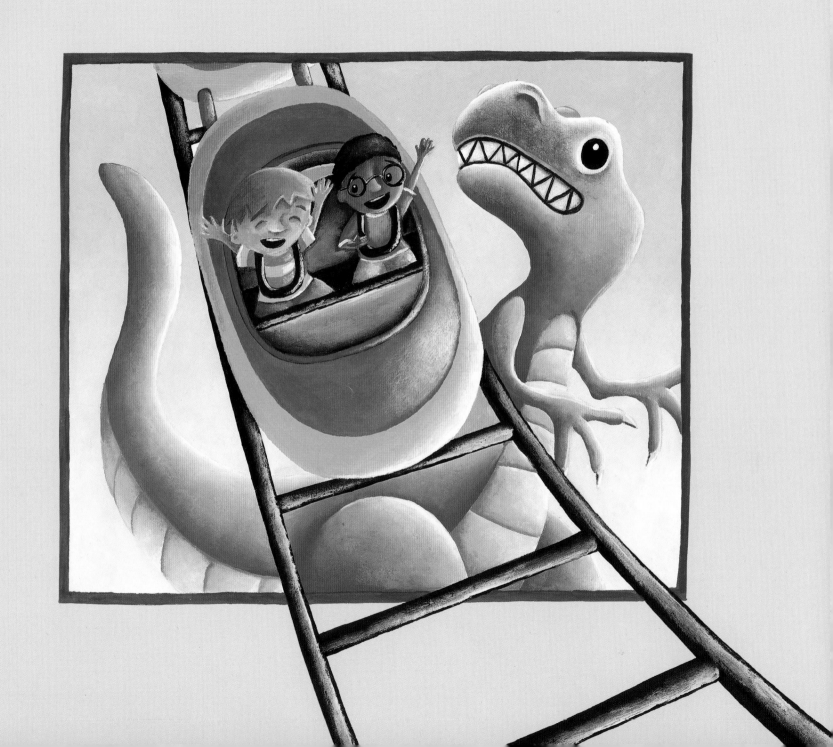